Curiosity Killed the Caterpillar

TAMARA STEINHUBL

Copyright © 2010 Tamara Steinhubl
All rights reserved.

ISBN: 1453659609
ISBN-13: 9781453659601
Library of Congress Control Number: 2010909543

Story by Tamara Steinhubl, MMFT

Tamara Steinhubl is a marriage and family therapist working with children and families in private practice in Winnipeg, Manitoba. Her specific interests and experience include working with trauma, transitional adjustments, parenting, abuse, grief/loss, depression, anxiety, disordered eating, addictions, family of origin issues, and attachment.

Illustrated by Geri Katopodis

Geri Katopodis received her Bachelor's of Art and Design from Columbia College Chicago in 2007. More of her work may be seen in Chicago galleries and through her website at www.garifalia.blogspot.com.

Preface

The intent of this story is to help grown-ups spark conversation with children about how they cope when difficult feelings come up, as well as for adults who are trying to make sense of terrible things that happened to them when they were hurt as a child. This is a children's story for grown-ups, or a story for grown-ups to read to a child.

Something terrible has happened to eleven-year-old Lucy. She is overwhelmed and confused and doesn't know what to do. So, she pushes all her Mad, Sad, Glad, and Scared, along with the Terrible Thing, into her backpack and runs away from home. On her journey, she meets many friends who share their experiences about how they cope and get through terrible things that have happened to them. All of these creatures teach valuable lessons for Lucy to add to her list of coping skills. Her journey helps her gather many skills and practice nurturing her precious self.

As opposed to using a "workbook" approach, this fictional story applies common themes in nature with coping and grounding techniques. This can provide concrete tools to self soothe and nurture your Self through difficult emotions.

Chapters

1. It Was A Terrible Thing That Had Happened ... 1
2. Lucy's Journal And Backpack ... 5
3. The Unforgettable Dream ... 11
4. A Ladybug's Love Is Unconditional ... 15
5. How Do You Feel Your Glad? ... 19
6. When You Let Go Of Scared, You Can Start To Trust ... 23
7. Snakes Can Find Comfort In Their New Skin ... 27
8. It Can Be Smart To Ask An Expert ... 33
9. Feeling Mad Doesn't Have To Be Bad ... 37
10. Trapped In A Cocoon ... 41
11. Snapdragons Are Wise And Brave ... 49
12. Yelling 'Ouch' Can Save Your Life ... 57
13. Sad Tells You There Is Love There ... 61
14. Taking The Risk To Come Out ... 65
15. Doing The Right Thing Can Be Difficult ... 67
16. When Taking A Rest Is Best ... 71
17. Reality Is Not Always What It Seems ... 73
18. Trust That The Universe Cares About You ... 77
19. A Magical Transformation ... 79
20. Lucy Finds Her *Self* ... 83
21. Lucy's Journal ... 87

1

It Was A Terrible Thing That Had Happened

Lucy wandered the house. She moved from room to room, aimlessly trying to find something. She didn't know what. She got lost in the staircase. She had been focusing blindly on a crack in the wall. Nobody seemed to understand. They told her that bad things happened to good people all the time. They told her that everyone experienced terrible things at some point in their lives and that eventually she'd get over it. They tried to reassure her that, in time, she would forget. Lucy couldn't do that. She sat in the corner, gazing out the window. She watched the raindrops slip and slide into one another and gather in a puddle on the windowsill. But, it wasn't raining outside; her eyes were leaking.

She looked at her reflection in the tears. She could see an image of her Self that was hurting badly. She wiped the tears away with her sleeve. She didn't want to look at her Self. It was horrible what had happened. She was angry, sad, mad, scared, and confused, and nobody could give her any answers. Nobody seemed to be able to tell her what to do.

Maybe it was her fault? Everyone wanted her to stop asking questions, or, better yet, to stop talking entirely. It wasn't fair. She must have done something to deserve this. Everyone wanted her to be happy again. They tried with placating

words that felt empty and hollow. They would distract her with activities, or movies, or talk about anything but the Terrible Thing that had happened. They didn't care. She tried not to care, too.

Lucy's head was spinning, and she felt sick to her stomach. It was like everyone around her was pretending it hadn't happened. Something had happened. Nothing made sense. Maybe she had turned invisible? Lucy didn't know how to move on. She didn't know how to deal with "it." She wanted to fly away from everyone. Since she didn't know how to fly, she decided to RUN. She decided to disappear far away into the forest where the butterflies fly and the flowers bloom. She dreamed of making her home in the forest. She could make friends with the animals. There, nobody would bother her, and she could be far away from the Terrible Thing that had happened.

2

Lucy's Journal And Backpack

Lucy grabbed her special journal and stuffed all of her feelings, along with the Terrible Thing, into her backpack. She stomped down the stairs and out the back door. She stood at the gate and yelled, "I HATE YOU ALL!" She started running. She ran until she found herself in the middle of the forest. Sweat was beading down her neck and back. She was out of breath, and her body felt tired. She found herself in a quiet spot, where nobody could find her. The backpack was such a heavy burden. Slipping it off, she felt lighter.

There were so many beautiful colors and sounds and smells of nature. Her fear of the unknown made her anxious. At the same time, she felt some peace with trusting her Self. She was glad to be away from everyone. Nobody was there to tell her to "get over it."

A stream trickled by, tickling her fingertips. She hopped along the rocks and worked her way to a magnificent tree. It was a tree like no other she had seen. A furry tree with long, soft leaves cascading all the way to the ground. It looked like a friendly furry monster that could provide good shelter and wouldn't turn on her. Gently pulling back the leaves, she crawled under its protective cover. Inside was quiet. She closed her eyes and listened, b-r-e-a-t-h-i-n-g in the smell of life around her. It was a pungent sweet smell.

Her top half felt so warm and sparkly. It was like an innocence echoing from the past, that now, felt very present. Her bottom half felt locked and numb. Her feet were tired from running. No matter how fast she had run, they hadn't let her soar into the sky to fly. She focused intently on her top half, remembering those who loved and held her in their hearts, even if they were not physically present. She felt what it had been like before the Terrible Thing. She imagined all the feel-good life-affirming energy of the forest embracing her. She smiled and hugged herself tight. Shy and giggling, she felt free, away from everyone telling her what to do and how to feel.

Lucy needed to remember this feeling, so she pulled out her journal from her backpack and wrote it down:

* Find a private space to sit quietly
* Feel the good life affirming energy surrounding me
* List out names of important people who love me
* Remember happier times

* Remind myself that I am loved
* Hug my Self
* Smell the fresh air

As it grew dark, she noticed the sounds of the forest changing. The birds began to settle, and their twittering was replaced by the chirping of crickets. Leaves gently rustled in the breeze. The grass felt cool underneath her fingers.

* Be aware of different sounds around me—listen carefully
* Feel the grass with my hands—feel the temperature and its softness

3

The Unforgettable Dream

Her body became more relaxed with each breath, and she drifted into a deep sleep. Even though her body was sleeping, her mind was wide awake. In her dream, images of the forest danced around her and she started running. This time, her feet moved so fast that she was able to take off into the sky. Jumping turned into flying in big leaps and bounds over trees and rivers. The feeling was exhilarating. Lucy felt free.

When she finally landed, she was stopped in her tracks by a Praying Mantis, who had an ominous look. She froze and stared at this creature. She knew that Praying Mantis was believed to have mystical powers and can either grant or take away life. It turned its head around until it was looking at her from behind itself (as if to show it could watch her from any direction). It had rows of long, sharp spikes along its front legs (as if to say it could seriously take hold of anything or anyone it desired). A struggle would surely mean death. She remembered hearing that the great martial artists of the world had learned many of their moves from the Praying Mantis. Although she had taken some beginner karate classes, she knew she was no match for this creature. She couldn't take her eyes off of it. Lucy was totally mesmerized.

Lucy began to tremble and tried to run away, but her feet no longer moved. She struggled and pushed, but her legs wouldn't work. She felt betrayed by her feet and legs, which no longer let her jump and fly free. As she cursed her lower limbs, she swore she heard Praying Mantis warn her not to cross its path again. She took the warning seriously. She awoke trying to shake the feeling of fear that was vibrating inside her bones.

She focused on her breathing and reached for her journal:

* Remind myself to breathe—and that it's going to be OK
* Beware of Terrible Things (Praying Mantis)
* Keep practicing karate

4

A Ladybug's Love Is Unconditional

Lucy shook her head and wiped the sleep from her eyes. Regaining her focus, she realized she was face-to-face with a Ladybug.

"What are you writing?" he asked.

"I'm writing down important things I need to remember."

"What are you doing here?"

She told him, "I came to get away from everyone and see where the butterflies fly and the flowers bloom. I would also like to learn how to fly high up into the sky."

He laughed and said, "You won't find any butterflies or flowers hiding under this tree. Hiding may keep you away from everyone, but then you won't see or learn very much."

"I'm scared to go out into this forest alone, but I feel safe under the protective cover of this big tree."

The Ladybug said, "You are safe and perfectly welcome here. I can fly. Let me show you the way."

Lucy had to explain that her feet prevented her from flying because they weighed her to the ground.

Again, he laughed. "You don't need feet to fly, but I can see that you are stuck."

They sat together for awhile trying to figure out how to work around this predicament.

"What's in the backpack?" asked the Ladybug.

"I keep my journal of important things to remember in there. I have also stuffed all my feelings inside of it, too."

"Oh," replied the Ladybug. "It looks extremely full and heavy. What kinds of feelings do you have inside your backpack?"

"Well," said Lucy, "I have a lot of Mad in there. There are also heaps of Scared and a great deal of Sad. And smooshed far down at the very bottom is a Terrible Thing I have buried in there, too."

"Wow. That *is* a heavy burden to carry," said the Ladybug.

5

How Do You Feel Your Glad?

The Ladybug thought for a moment. "You know, there are many different kinds of feelings. It seems you forgot to mention one. Where do you keep your Glad?"

Lucy smiled and answered quickly, "I keep my Glad inside with me!"

"You do seem happy," said the Ladybug.

"How can you tell?"

"Your body seems relaxed, calm, and you are smiling. When you answered me, your face lit up, and you sounded excited. Now the question is, how do you experience this happy feeling?"

"What do you mean?" asked Lucy.

"Check in with your Self," encouraged the Ladybug. "Close your eyes and take a few breaths. Be aware of what you feel inside your body. Where do you feel happiness in your body? What does it feel like? How big is it?"

Lucy took a deep breath and tried to figure out where she felt this feeling. It seemed to live in her face when she smiled, and in her chest, near her heart. She placed her hand over her heart and held it there a moment. She could feel a glimmering energy inside her body, like happy sparkles sending electric smiles to her face.

The Ladybug went on, "There are many different kinds of happy, and it's a pleasant feeling that can help guide your way. It's important to listen to what this feeling is telling you because, when you follow your heart, it will help you discover things in life that make you feel good. You could feel any emotion from mildly amused, contented, pleased, or satisfied… all the way up to the biggest of happiness, which would be supreme joy and bliss!"

Lucy smiled as she remembered the feeling of exhilaration in her dream, when she could let go her feet to fly.

The Ladybug went on, "We have all sorts of different things that make us feel good. It's important to know what makes our Self happy. That will help us learn how to make important decisions and how to take gentle care of ourselves, too. What do you need to feel more happiness?" asked the Ladybug.

Lucy was glad to have met the Ladybug. She shared with him that she would be super duper happy if she could just learn to fly. She told him about her dream and how, if she could fly, all of her problems could be solved. She reasoned that anytime something bad happened, she could stuff all the bad feelings in her backpack and fly away from whoever or whatever was bothering her.

"Ummm, it doesn't quite work that way," said the Ladybug.

"Why not?" asked Lucy. "It's good to be happy, isn't it?"

"Of course, but the thing about feelings is that they are not 'good' or 'bad' or 'right' or 'wrong'. They are just helpful information. Feelings can be pleasant or unpleasant…or *really* pleasant, or *really* unpleasant…or *really really* pleasant, or *really really unpleasant*."

Lucy glanced at her backpack hoping the Ladybug wouldn't notice.

Then, the Ladybug said, "What kinds of important information are you missing out on because you have all those other feelings zipped up tightly in that backpack? If you hide them, you are hiding your Self away, just like you are hiding under this tree. What wonderful things are we missing out on knowing about you if you keep so much stuffed away? You will never be free to fly if you carry such heavy burdens on your back."

"I'm not ready to open my backpack yet," said Lucy.

"That's OK," said the Ladybug. "You are not alone. You don't have to carry this burden all by yourself anymore. Everything is going to be fine."

Lucy whipped out her journal again:

* Be aware of what I'm feeling in my body
* It's important to notice what feels good
* Do things that feel good to take gentle care of myself
* Remind myself that I am not alone

Ladybugs are well known for their ability to bring luck and to help people find their way. He looked thoughtfully at Lucy and told her, "More heads are better than one. Let's get out from under this tree and see what we can find."

"Can I ask you something first?" Lucy asked.

Ladybug said, "Of course."

"Have you heard of any Praying Mantis in this area?"

"Oh, yes," replied Ladybug. "They can be unpredictable, so always be on the lookout. They are hard to see because they blend into their surroundings and can be soooo still and silent. If you see one, be sure to change your direction."

Lucy looked around warily. "Are you afraid of the Praying Mantis?" asked Lucy.

"Well, I am not tasty to Praying Mantis," replied Ladybug. "They are not too interested in bothering with me because I let out a stinky smell that tastes really bad."

"Like a skunk?" asked Lucy.

"Sort of," replied the Ladybug. "If we come across a Praying Mantis, I will try to reason with it and protect you."

Lucy was reminded of other times when people had promised to protect her and be there for her, and they hadn't followed through. For the first time, she felt like she didn't trust the Ladybug either. But, she figured she would believe him. He did seem to know what he was talking about, and he was her only friend in the forest. Although the Ladybug tried to reassure Lucy that he could reason with any Praying Mantis, she was still worried.

6

When You Let Go Of Scared, You Can Start To Trust

Lucy's forehead furrowed.

"I notice that your body is tense, and your eyes are wide. Your forehead is all scrunched up, and you keep looking around. Are you scared?" asked the Ladybug.

Lucy glared at her backpack again. The scared feeling she'd stuffed in there must have gotten out. It was written all over her face. Her eyebrows were raised up tightly, forming a crease in the middle of her forehead. She felt like there was a knot in her stomach, pulsating in nervous bursts. She was pulling at her hair and picking her fingernails. She was scared to leave the protective cover of the big furry tree. "How could feeling scared possibly be helpful?" Lucy asked. "It is *really* unpleasant."

The Ladybug encouraged her to take a couple deep breaths and explained, "There are many different kinds of scared. Some scared feelings can be pleasant. Like if someone surprises you with something special, or if you're on a fun ride in an amusement park. Some scared feelings can be unpleasant, like feeling anxious, worried, and fearful. Sometimes scared feelings can be so unpleasant that your body may even freeze in shock and terror."

Lucy flashed back to her dream about the Praying Mantis. She had been completely immobilized, as though her body was pulling her back but wasn't moving at the same time. It was exactly like freezing in terror, she thought.

The Ladybug went on, "Despite how unpleasant this feeling might be, it's important because it gets your attention and is there to protect you. It makes you take notice of your surroundings and figure out how to make yourself feel safe. As with the Praying Mantis…if you see one, what can you do to protect yourself?"

Lucy imagined herself alone in the forest to figure out what she would do. "Well, I could walk in the other direction, maybe pick up my pace. I could either hide or make lots of noise—they probably don't like lots of noise. I could call out for you, or someone, to try to reason with it."

"Very good," replied the Ladybug.

Lucy added, "My mind can think of things to do now, but that didn't help in my dream when I froze. It was like something else took control of my body. I was all alone in the big forest."

"Trust your body," said the Ladybug. "Your body tells you what you are feeling. Feelings don't always make sense right away, but they are always there for a reason. I'm sure you froze because that was the right thing to do in that moment. Sometimes staying still and silent can shield you from being noticed. Other times, running as fast as you can and making lots of noise will protect you. It depends on the circumstances, and each situation can be different."

Ladybug encouraged Lucy to be curious about what her feelings were telling her. He said it was good to talk about what she noticed with someone she trusted.

Lucy began to feel reassured and less anxious. Interestingly, her backpack seemed to be a little lighter, too. She reached for her journal:

- Remember to B-R-E-A-T-H-E
- More heads are better than one
- I can yell to someone I trust for help
- Trust what my body is saying
- Be curious about what the feeling is trying to tell me
- Talk about my feelings with someone I can trust

7

Snakes Can Find Comfort In Their New Skin

Venturing out into the woods together, a Snake slithered by to say hello. "You two look like you're up to something," remarked the Snake.

"Do you know anything about the Praying Mantis?" asked Lucy.

The Snake told them, "It is very rare to find one, but if you do, it will be the last thing you see. The Praying Mantis is calm and patient; it never makes a move unless it is completely sure of itself. I'm not even sure if I believe they really exist."

"Of course they exist," whispered Ladybug to Lucy. "Praying Mantis has been known to eat snakes. Sometimes snakes will pretend there is no danger to make themselves feel safe."

This sounded like a strange way to make oneself feel protected. Surely it would be better to know where the danger lurked and to try to stay away from it. It reminded Lucy of everyone back home pretending that the Terrible Thing hadn't really happened. Maybe that was their way of protecting themselves, too.

"Snakes are smart creatures," said Ladybug. "If we were to worry about every possible thing that could hurt us out there, we would be too afraid to go out at all."

Lucy was realizing that, even though she was far away from where the Terrible Thing had happened, danger could be found anywhere. She clutched her backpack and wrote in her journal:

* Try not to worry too much
* There are different ways to cope with Terrible Things
* Listen to what my body signals are saying and trust I'll know what I need

The Snake asked what they were doing there and why they were so curious about Praying Mantis.

Lucy told him about her dream and her backpack. She told him that she had to learn how to move on from Terrible Things that happen and that she was certain that being able to fly would help her do this.

"Ah," said the Snake, "a Terrible Thing happens to me every few months. You see, I spend my days finding imbalance in the ecosystem and work towards restoring that balance. This is difficult work that requires a lot of concentration and attention to what is going on around me. I have to think and focus until there is so much information inside my mind that my body starts to feel heavy and burdened. I feel a bubbling swell within me, and I become itchy and restless. It becomes too difficult to concentrate on anything else. My skin buzzes and starts to feel uncomfortable—it aches and pulls at me. The first time it happened, I was so scared because I thought my body was being tied in knots and that I might literally explode!"

The Snake went on, "Tension grows along my body, and I just want to get it off me! It feels disgusting. The only thought left in my head is 'Get it off! Ewwww, yucky blech! Get me out of here!'."

"That sounds terrible!" said Lucy. "How do you deal with such an unpleasant feeling?"

The Snake replied, "Sometimes I can find an Aloe plant and wrap myself around it, letting its natural oils lessen the itchiness. Sometimes I go for a dip into the river and let the cool waters soothe me. Other times, I grit my teeth and hiss loudly to give sound to the discomfort. That can ease the irritation sometimes. But, eventually, I keep growing and start to swell out of my skin, and there is no stopping it. So, there comes a time when it gets too painful, itchy, and heavy, and I have to accept that change is coming. I need to slither around, stretch, and shuffle until I'm right out of it."

Lucy could relate to that horrible feeling. Since the Terrible Thing had happened to her, she was having trouble concentrating as well. Sometimes, she would feel so full of confusion and hurt that her skin literally began to ache, too. The Snake was good at noticing what happened in his body. She reached for her journal again:

The Snake reassured Lucy, "Now, each time it happens, I can trust that there's a new skin waiting for me when I get out. It feels so fresh and renewed, and I breathe in the feeling of this new, comforting skin embracing me."

* When I feel uncomfortable in my skin, I can use moisturizer with Aloe
* Have a nice bath in cool water
* Move my body
* Make a sound out loud (like hissing or saying Eww or Yucky Blech!)

Lucy thought, maybe a way to move on could be for her to get a new skin…maybe then her feet would learn to propel herself to fly. Maybe she could hiss the feeling out of her. So, she lay on the ground and concentrated on her shuffling and hissing and Blickety Blech Blarghing! Wiggling every which way, she tried to will herself out of her unpleasant feeling and her heavy feet.

Just then, a Bird flew by, squawking, "You're doing it all wrong! If you want to fly, you need to look to where you want to go, concentrate, and flap your *upper* limbs."

It seemed rude to Lucy that this Bird just swooped in and started screeching orders, interrupting her concentration. She flashed it a crooked look.

8

It Can Be Smart To Ask An Expert

The Ladybug and Snake told Lucy that if she wanted to learn to fly, then it might be helpful to listen to Bird's advice. After all, birds are experts in flying.

Reluctantly, Lucy said, "I need you to answer a question for me first."

"Fine," snapped the Bird. "What's your question?"

"What do you know about the Praying Mantis?"

The Bird cocked her head to one side and warned, "You stay away from those things. If you see one, fly away as fast as you can. The Praying Mantis ate my cousin, the Hummingbird. It was a Terrible Thing that happened. Fortunately, I am much bigger than my cousin, so I don't have such problems. I also have better eyesight with which to see Praying Mantis—despite how good they are at camouflage. I can see one right over there, but you have no need to worry; it is far away."

Lucy felt intimidated. This Bird seemed to know everything. Lucy felt even more pressure to learn how to fly now. She thanked the Snake for taking the time to tell his experience, and she told him how much she appreciated his sharing.

"No problem-o!" said the Snake as he slithered away. "It feels good to help others. It's part of restoring balance." He had to get back to work stabilizing the ecosystem anyway.

She quickly noted in her journal before she could forget:

* It's OK to ask for help from an expert
* Be strong and ask questions, even if you are feeling intimidated
* It's good to help others
* Share what you know
* Let others share what they know
* Find balance and stability
* Remember to say thank you

"Well," cheeped the Bird sarcastically, "are you going to sit and write all day, or do you want to learn how to fly?" Bird launched into a big explanation involving flapping, singing, concentrating, and elaborate swooshing.

Lucy decided to take the Bird's advice and try. She stood up and began flapping her arms, faster and faster, harder and harder. In the strongest voice she could muster, she sang loudly, "Give me the strength to fly high up into the sky!" She was doing everything Bird told her to do. If she concentrated any harder, she thought her mind might explode. Other than starting to sweat and feeling silly, her feet weighed her to the ground and refused to soar upward.

Bird was zooming and swooping, soaring high circles above their heads, singing, "You're thinking too much, sing and be free like meeee!"

Lucy felt discouraged, flopped back on the ground, and grabbed her journal:

* Don't give up
* Concentrate and focus on what I want to happen
* Show off a little
* Sing loudly

"What are you writing *now*?" chirped the Bird.

Lucy shoved her journal into her backpack and said, "Even though it didn't work, it might be valuable to remember." She didn't tell the Bird that she enjoyed listening to her singing and watching her fly—she wasn't feeling friendly towards this Bird who was showing off and tweeting orders.

"Writing things down helps me remember important stuff—especially when I'm having trouble concentrating," replied Lucy defensively.

Bird continued swooping and swishing in the sky and sang out, "Don't bother with concentration! Look at Meeeee. Tweet and flap your upper limbs, have fun, and just do it like this—fly!"

Bird was making Lucy feel mad and incompetent.

9

Feeling Mad Doesn't Have To Be Bad

"You seem angry, Lucy," said the Ladybug. "Your brow is furrowed and your nose is scrunched up. You are huffing and puffing, and your fists are clenched. What is your body telling you?"

Lucy glared at her backpack. Was it possible that another feeling escaped and went into her body again? She checked in with her body and her Self. She did feel an increasing energy vibrating from her belly up to her chest, and she wanted to yell and stomp her feet. Her arms were tingling like she wanted to hit something. She felt as though she might lose her temper. She had angry, hateful thoughts and was trying to contain her breathing so that she did not blow up.

"You're right," replied Lucy sharply. "But how can feeling mad possibly be *good*?"

The Ladybug calmly reminded her, "Remember, feelings are pleasant or unpleasant. They are not 'good' or 'bad'. Your body is speaking to you. Mad can be big or small, too. You could just be in a grumpy mood. Learning something new can be frustrating when you don't get it right in the first few tries. You may feel more annoyed, silent, or even so furiously mad that you think hateful things and want to lash out at yourself or someone else. It's OK to feel these things, but you are responsible for what you do with these feelings. For example, you can be really angry, but it is not OK to hurt yourself or someone else."

"How can anger possibly be *helpful*?" asked an exasperated Lucy.

"Well, it can make you feel stronger and more powerful. It can give you energy to motivate you to change something that doesn't feel right. It can also tell you that something unfair has happened or let you know that someone has come too close and you want them to back off."

Lucy threw her backpack on the ground and fumed. There was nothing breakable inside, so she figured it was OK. Surely, the zipper was broken for all these feelings to be slipping back into her. "Stupid backpack! Stupid feelings!" She gave it an extra hard squish, squash, and mash with her hands.

"What is making you so angry right now?" asked the Ladybug.

Lucy could feel her voice shaking and getting louder as she explained that she didn't like the Bird being rude and ordering her around. She felt like the Bird was mocking her and telling her she wasn't trying hard enough. She got up and started pacing, stomping her feet and kicking some rocks because she had been trying hard. She felt like the Bird was showing off and rubbing it in her face that she couldn't fly. She so desperately wanted to learn and felt so useless. It reminded her of the Terrible Thing that had happened, and how everyone back home was pretending that everything was fine when it wasn't. She wanted to throw her backpack at the stupid Bird (but she didn't because it's not OK to hurt someone else). She started making angry sounds instead: "Grrr, arrrghh, phhfftt, maaahhhhhh, grrraaaaahhhhhh!"

"You see," said the Ladybug, "this is important information. This is getting you closer to how you truly feel. Look at your backpack; it's getting a little smaller, and I bet it's also lighter."

Lucy admitted that she felt some relief after letting herself vent.

- If I am angry I can stomp my feet and yell
- I can ask the one I am angry with to back off
- Vent to somebody about why I am angry
- I cannot hurt myself or someone else
- I can hit, kick, or throw my backpack (as long as there's nothing breakable inside)

Unbeknownst to Lucy, Bird was watching all of this from a tree branch above. Bird was just being a bird and hadn't intended to upset Lucy.

"Tweeter tweet tweet?" said Bird sweetly, trying to get Lucy's attention.

Lucy glared up suspiciously.

"Can you please forgive me?" asked Bird. "I was honestly trying to help. I wish you would have told me directly how I made you feel. I don't realize how easy it is for me to fly, and sometimes I get carried away by how much fun it can be. I get lost in the moment. I forget that it's different for humans."

Lucy believed the Bird was being sincere. She felt compassion expanding within her arms and chest. It was a warm feeling of calm and relief that felt as though it were pulling her to feel Bird's point of view. Lucy realized that she was learning how to trust her instincts and what her body was telling her. She told Bird, "Yes, of course I forgive you." She also apologized for not telling her more openly, and that in the future, she would try to do so. They smiled at one another.

* Find compassion for others
* Be willing to consider forgiveness
* If I have a problem with someone, I should try to work it out with them directly

10

Trapped In A Cocoon

When Lucy looked back up at the Bird to share what she learned, she saw a cocoon secured tightly on the tree branch. "Look beside you!" she yelled excitedly. She had never seen a cocoon in real life. As she peered up at it, it began to vibrate.

"Hello in there. What's going on?" she called out.

A muffled voice explained, "I was a beautiful striped caterpillar. Mmff mmff. My job was to just eat and eat to my hearts content. I picked the healthiest and most tasty leaves and ate them up. Mmff mmff. I would meander around finding good things to take in and eat. My body just grew and grew, and it was delightful because it showed I was absorbing healthy things around me, and I was so happy. The more I ate, the more I grew. Mmff mmff. Then one day, I became tired and needed to digest in peace. I heard rumblings in the forest about a Praying Mantis being near, and I didn't want it to find me, so I spun this cocoon around my body to keep me safe and allow me to rest. Mmff mmff."

Lucy could relate to the voice in the cocoon needing to hide to feel safe from unpleasant things.

"You know about Praying Mantis?" Lucy asked.

"Oh, yes," replied the voice. "I think that is how I got into this mess trying to protect myself from it!"

"Then what happened?" Lucy asked.

The voice in the cocoon went on, "I slept for a long time. When I awoke, I didn't know what had happened to me! I don't know what I am anymore! This is so frightening. Maybe if I didn't eat so much. Maybe if I didn't take so much in. Maybe if I didn't spin this cocoon."

Lucy realized that what used to be a Caterpillar in this cocoon was troubled. She grabbed her journal and frantically reviewed her list of things to try and help. She read aloud, *"Maybe you could try to B-R-E-A-T-H-E. Trust what your body is doing. Be curious about what might be happening. Try to make a noise that sounds like the feeling."*

The voice inside let out stifled yips and agonizing bellows. It was hard for them to hear this poor creature in so much pain.

Bird explained that this was all part of nature's plan for the Caterpillar. "She would start out a Caterpillar, spin a cocoon, and eventually emerge as a Butterfly."

Lucy asked, "What's happening to the Caterpillar right now, in this moment?"

The Caterpillar cried, "Yes! That's what I want to know mmff mmff. What is happening to me in here? What do I do?"

The Bird told them that she wasn't really a Caterpillar anymore…more like a Caterfly…or a Butterpillar (half Caterpillar and half Butterfly). "The cocoon is the protective shell that allows for this transformation to occur. It is important to remain curious to this magical event. What colors might you turn out to be? How high will you be able to fly? Will you recognize your other Caterpillar friends when they join you as Butterflies, too?"

The Ladybug suddenly got an idea. He flew up to the Caterfly…or Butterpillar…and said, "We know you are going through something very difficult and unpleasant, but you may be able to help our friend, Lucy. She is carrying such a heavy backpack and needs to know how to let go of her feet in order to fly."

Muffled sounds and shifts rippled from the cocoon, and two angry eyes poked out. "It is terrible what is happening in here! I have lost all my suction-cupped feet, and my body is changing shape; it is very painful! I am scared for what is busting through my bloody back! It is dreadful, and I am miserable! I can't believe you are even asking me such a thing. Go away! I am too busy and burdened myself to explain anything. I will find my curiosity somehow in this confusion, but it's messy, and I do not want to talk to anybody right now!"

It felt unpleasant to be yelled at and told 'no', but Lucy could relate to feeling angry and not wanting to speak with anyone. She also knew from her journal's list of important things that it was healthy to vent and tell people to back off if you needed space. She didn't mean to cause the Caterfly…or Butterpillar…any more grief.

The Ladybug explained, "Sometimes when we are in pain, we can lash out at others, and it's important to try to be compassionate, kind, and to respect others' need for privacy."

Lucy wanted to help. She was curious about what would happen to the Caterfly…or Butterpillar, too. At the same time, she was clear and certain that she wanted to be left alone. So Lucy would just have to muster up some patience. Patience was harder to find. Connecting to her patience meant focusing on her breathing and redirecting her energy towards her own struggle. Lucy looked at her journal again and decided to add:

* Remember to eat healthy and tasty things
* Recognize my beauty
* Try to stay curious about what is happening
* Be compassionate and kind
* It's OK to tell others I can't talk right now
* Respect the need for privacy for both your Self and others
* Be patient

So, Lucy, the Ladybug, and the Bird decided to give the Caterfly…or Butterpillar…some privacy and continue on their way.

The tall trees began to part, and there was a big clearing full of different kinds of beautiful flowers to smell and admire. The ground was smattered with glorious colors. They seemed to cry out their own unique fragrance in silent roars. Some were spicy and others blunt. Some were harsh and others gentle. Lucy wanted to sniff them all! Nature is very creative, she thought. I would like to be more creative, too.

11

Snapdragons Are Wise And Brave

The trio started to play an exciting game of "I Spy With My Little Eye." They were naming all sorts of colors, different kinds of flowers, and laughing loudly. Thoughts about the Praying Mantis seemed far away from everyone's mind. Lucy loved learning new words—especially when she could watch them grow—Alliums, Trilliums, Lilies, Hydrangeas, Pansies, Snapdragons…to name only a few.

If Lucy found herself thinking about the Terrible Thing that had happened, she would take a deep inhaling s-n-i-f-f of one of these flowers, and the scent would bring her back to the present. When she started thinking bad thoughts, she could name each color, each flower, and try to remember its scent. She picked her favorite (Pansy) and tucked it carefully away in her backpack.

They stopped to rest for a moment, and Lucy pulled out her journal:

* Remember to laugh loud and play
* Try to be spontaneous
* Learn new words
* Be creative like nature
* Stop to smell the flowers and other things around me
* Name all the different things I notice and see

As they sniffed and giggled, a Snapdragon piped up. "It's so nice to hear sounds of playing and laughter in this clearing. What are you writing about?"

Lucy explained that she was learning important things from all her friends in the forest, and she wanted to write them all down so she wouldn't forget.

"I can see how much you appreciate all the different fragrances of flowers in this clearing. I have a story you might like," said the Snapdragon.

They all gathered round and listened intently.

Snapdragon eagerly began sharing with them. "This clearing had once been only grasses. Great winds came and brought all sorts of seeds to this clearing. Over the seasons, those seeds worked their way deep down into the soil. I recall my Self as a seed, having to let go into the unknown to risk blooming."

"It was very lonely as a seed surrounded by thick soil. It was so dark, and I could not see anything. It was silent and suffocating, and I felt trapped and panicky. The fear turned into a deep stirring inside, an energy that forced me to push through and up and out, despite the weight on top of me. I was pushing, pulling, banging, and knocking. I felt like I was beating myself up against the hard walls of the seed shell. I was just about to give up when something told me that all I had to do was 'Follow the warmth and affection of the sun.' I felt around and found a spot that was warmer than the rest. That is where I decided to push. I had found a weakness in the wall!"

"It was very brave of you to push through the soil when you couldn't even see what was ahead," said Lucy.

"Yes," agreed the Snapdragon. "It is no different from all these other flowers you see around us. We all had to take the risk to venture out into the unknown. Some of us didn't make it. Some were too frightened to poke their heads out, so they withered and died. Some gave up before even finding the soft spot. Some poked through but didn't fully bloom. We all smell different. Some people like our smells and others make them sneeze and wheeze."

Lucy could relate with this idea. She had felt scared to leave the protective cover of the tree when she had first entered the forest. As she met new friends along the way, a part of her worried if they would accept her as she was.

* Use my energy to keep pushing forward even when it's dark
* Feel the warmth of the sun on my face
* Be brave and courageous
* Risk showing my true self, even if it's different from others
* Trust that I am important in my own special ways

12

Yelling 'Ouch' Can Save Your Life

Bird started getting hungry and began to sniff for worms. She found a tasty fat one burrowing into the soil. She wasn't fast enough though and just snipped off his bottom half.

"Delicious!" and she smacked her beak.

"OUCH!" the worm yelled.

Lucy looked confused and did a double-take. "Wait, how come you are not dead? Bird ate half of you!"

Bird burped.

The Worm laughed and said, "I am so important to making nutrients in the soil that my body is designed in segments to regenerate." He explained, "It was extremely painful at first (hence the need to yell OUCH), but then I would concentrate hard on the part that hurt, and concentrate breathing all of that negative energy out. In my case, kind of like breathing out my butt. Eventually, I trust it will heal. I always grow a new bottom, so there is no need to worry."

Well, Lucy certainly felt segmented, and she still didn't know how to let go of her feet to fly. Everything she'd tried so far hadn't worked. She thought this Worm had the answer.

"Maybe you could cut me in half so I could r-e-g-e-n-e-r-a-t-e?"

All the animals started to roll on the ground laughing. It was such a far-fetched idea. She even started laughing at her Self. When she finally stopped giggling, she jotted down in her journal:.

* Imagine breathing all the negative energy out of the part of my body that hurts
* It's important to be able to laugh at my Self

Lucy asked Worm, "How do you find your way around in the soil? A Snapdragon told us that it's terribly dark and heavy, and you can't see anything under there. She said that it was frightening to risk bursting from a seed through the soil to the sun."

"Ahh," replied the worm, "that is another part of my job. It doesn't matter much that I can't see. I sense things by just feeling my way through the earth. I don't feel any weight on top of me, and I just focus on digging deep enough so I can softly encourage the seeds to follow the warmth and affection of the sun."

"Just like Snapdragon had said!" They all gasped in unison.

"Yes, all who inhabit Mother Earth are connected in important ways," replied the Worm. "Big or small, we are all interconnected. We just have to focus on being true to our Self and remember to follow our five senses: seeing, hearing, feeling/touching, taste, and smell. Our purpose will become clear, even if others don't recognize it."

Lucy's body seemed to change posture into one that felt more powerful. Maybe her backpack was becoming lighter. Perhaps it was because she had gathered so much good information in her journal, information that she was getting good at practicing. She realized that, even though all of her friends in the forest were different, they all had an important purpose—and everyone did seem to be linked together in important ways.

13

Sad Tells You There Is Love There

Lucy began to feel a yearning for home. Despite the Terrible Thing that had happened, she missed her connections to her family and friends and home. Her eyes started to well up, and her body slumped.

"What's happening?" Lucy said to her Self. "A moment ago, I was feeling stronger, and now I am feeling fragile and weak."

"It's OK to be vulnerable. You seem really sad all of a sudden," said the Ladybug.

She checked in with her Self. This time, sadness must have leaked out of her backpack and into her body. She felt her bottom lip beginning to quiver, and her heart ached in her chest. Her body felt heavy, and her breaths were more like sighs. A lump formed in her throat, and she couldn't swallow it. Her sinuses felt stuffed up and tingly. Memories of the Terrible Thing came flooding back. Lucy began to cry.

"This feeling is so unpleasant," she whimpered. "How could sadness possibly be helpful?"

"Well," Ladybug explained, "sadness can be big or small, too, depending on the situation. There might be something that touches your heart and makes you feel compassion or empathy. Or, maybe the sadness is bigger and feels lonely or depressing…all the way to the biggest sad of all: the ache and

sting of gut-wrenching grief." The Ladybug went on to explain that, "Sadness helps you to know something meaningful or significant is lost, gone, dead, or missing. It tells you that love is still there in your heart.

"What is making you sad now?" asked the Ladybug.

Between sobs, Lucy managed to say that "My backpack is all opened up, and all the feelings stored in there have been spilling into me! I hadn't meant to open the backpack, but all I can think of is the Terrible Thing." Big round tears started spilling out of her eyes, and she wailed as her body shook.

Bird swooped down and landed on Lucy's shoulder. She gently wrapped one wing around Lucy's cheek and wiped away her tears. Lucy snuggled in. Her feathers felt so soft and comforting.

"It's going to be OK," said the Ladybug in a calm, soothing voice. "Your needs are OK. What can we do to help?"

Lucy took a deep breath and thought hard. She finally managed to say, "I might be ready to start finding my way back home."

14

Taking The Risk To Come Out

So off they went to retrace their steps through the forest. They found themselves back at the spot where the cocoon had been. Lucy could see that the Caterfly...or Butterpillar...was on the verge of becoming a full-fledged Butterfly.

The Butterfly called out to get their attention, "Excuse me, kind Lucy. I'm sorry I was so harsh with you on our last meeting. I was very confused and frightened. I seem to be stuck. Could you please reach up and open my cocoon just a little bit with your strong fingers?"

Lucy could see the Butterfly was in pain, and she could relate. She felt compassion for the poor creature and wanted to help.

Butterfly sounded angry, "I was foolish to listen to you before! I used my curiosity like you suggested and now look at me. I'm so stuck. And I'm no longer a beautiful striped Caterpillar."

"Curiosity *did* kind of kill the Caterpillar, didn't it?" joked Bird.

Lucy stared angrily at the Bird. "This is no time for teasing," she snapped. "Curiosity helped the Caterpillar, erm Caterfly, erm Butterpillar...to transform itself into a beautiful Butterfly. She's almost out. Maybe I could open up the cocoon just an eensie beensie bit to help ease the pressure for her and make it easier?"

"Oh no," interrupted Bird, "you can't do that! The Caterpillar is *supposed* to change into a Butterfly. She needs to struggle out of her cocoon to squeeze all the excess liquid from her body to make it lean, light, and aerodynamic. Emerging from a cocoon is a painful process, and she is distressed and frustrated, but it needs to be done. It's important to allow the struggling. This will strengthen and toughen her wings—or else she won't be able to fly."

Lucy called up to Butterfly to try again, "You can do it!"

The Butterfly twisted and contorted a little more and said louder, "Don't you see? NO, I can't! Please, you are so big and strong, it would be nothing for you to just reach up and open the cocoon a little more. I just want to get out of here!"

15

Doing The Right Thing Can Be Difficult

Lucy had learned to trust nature's methods, even if they were difficult to watch sometimes. She reached for her journal and read out loud, *"Concentrate and focus on what you want until you believe it can happen. Use your energy to keep pushing forward. Feel the warmth of the sun on your face. Be brave. Risk showing your true Self! Be curious about what it will be like to fly!* I'm sorry you are in so much pain, Butterfly. I know you can do this!"

The Butterfly got angry and huffed, "You are not kind at all. In fact, you are being cruel! I'm in so much pain and clearly stuck, and you won't even use your strength to help a poor, feeble Butterfly? How can you expect me to fly when I have never done it before? You must be heartless!"

Lucy felt dismayed. Ladybug encouraged her to keep practicing what she'd learned.

So she took another deep breath and tried to cheer the Butterfly on, "Concentrate! Use your anger to push yourself out of this situation! Wiggle and stretch right out! Stay curious about what might happen next! We are here for you!"

The Butterfly grew even angrier and shouted, "I am the one in this stupid cocoon, and I am the one who knows it's too small! If you could just reach up and open it a little bit. It hurts! It hurts! It hurts so much, and you don't even care! I HATE YOU!"

Lucy, the Ladybug, and the Bird pulled up a log, sat down, and tried to think of ideas together. They felt bad for the Butterfly who was hurting and so angry. At the same time, they knew they couldn't grant the Butterfly's request. They didn't like being told they were hated—even if it was being said out of frustration. At the same time, they felt compassion and wanted to find a way to help.

Lucy also felt a pang of guilt in her stomach. She remembered the last words she had shouted when she left home to run away into the forest. She had said, "I HATE YOU," too. She hadn't meant it. She was just angry. It felt like so long ago now. Lucy had learned that sometimes you just have to let someone go through hard feelings. The Ladybug had taught her that feelings, even if they are unpleasant, are there for a reason to try to help you somehow. Lucy reached deep down into her heart and mustered up all the compassion she could. She looked up at the Butterfly and told her what she *could* do. "I can make sure no Squirrels come. I'll shoo them away."

The Butterfly huffed and puffed and got angrier; soon, she was struggling and screaming and *crickle crackle crick* she felt a little break in the cocoon. She wriggled and stretched her butterfly shoulders and shook about some more. Her anger afforded her some energy, which helped her widen the space.

Lucy jumped up. "See? Keep stretching! S-T-R-E-T-C-H! That seems to be working. You *can* do this, Butterfly!"

The Butterfly continued until she was completely spent.

16

When Taking A Rest Is Best

Bird interjected, "You have been working so hard. Maybe try taking a rest. I can sing to you as you take a break to build up more energy for the next part of your struggle."

As the Butterfly rested, Lucy thought that maybe that's what everyone back home was trying to do for her. Maybe they were trying to let her go through her own struggle about the Terrible Thing. Maybe she had needed to run away to get a rest, too?

* It can be good to let others learn how to do things on their own
* Remember to take rests
* S-T-R-E-T-C-H my body

When the butterfly had rested and had enough energy to wiggle and writhe again *flicker crackle snap*, she finally broke free! She stretched out her new wings and flapped them softly, getting used to her new body. Her anger melted into pride and accomplishment! She had done it! It wasn't until she was flying that she realized they had done her the most loving act in not helping her crack open the cocoon. And, wow, could she FLY. She swooped and fluttered about before landing on Lucy's shoulder, whispering a heartfelt "thank you" into her ear.

Lucy felt happy for the Butterfly. It did feel good to help others. Yet, her bottom lip stuck out as she looked down and kicked a few leaves.

Ladybug asked, "What is it, Lucy?"

"The Caterpillar was able to let go her suction-cupped feet to turn into a Butterfly and fly. She had a hundred feet, and I only have two. I still can't fly. I've tried everything. I've tried anything and everything, and I still don't know how to fly. I have failed."

17

Reality Is Not Always What It Seems

Just then, the Praying Mantis appeared before them. He caught them by surprise with his ominous look, exactly like Lucy remembered in her dream.

The Ladybug stepped in front of Lucy protectively and said firmly, "What do you want?"

Bird started squawking warning signals to all the other animals in the forest that Praying Mantis was near.

Praying Mantis began to speak. "I mean none of you any harm. I am very misunderstood. I have been watching you, Lucy, and I needed to let you have your struggle, just like you let the Butterfly. Have you not learned anything in your time in the forest?"

Lucy became defensive. "Of course I have learned!" She grabbed her journal and shook it in the direction of the Praying Mantis. "I have learned *lots*!"

"What did you come here for?" Praying Mantis asked.

Lucy thought hard. "I came to get away from the Terrible Thing and everyone telling me to get over it. I came to see where the butterflies fly and the flowers bloom. I came to make new friends in the forest. I came to learn how to fly. I have accomplished everything except…my feet still weigh me to the ground. I cannot fly."

Praying Mantis said, "I am much feared in this forest, but I have an important job, too. My purpose is to grant or take away life."

"Are…are…are you going to kill us?" asked Lucy in a shaky voice.

"Not in the way you are thinking," said Praying Mantis. "I help to embrace endings. An ending can be a kind of death. Sometimes it's messy. You can choose to risk coming out and living your life, or you can choose to run away and hide. It is up to you to decide. If you are willing to end an old way of being, it makes way for healing and the miracles of growth. It takes more courage to face your feelings than it does to stuff them away. It takes more strength to deal with Terrible Things that happen than it does to shove them deep down into your backpack. You cannot be empowered without taking responsibility for what you need and how you feel. Empower your Self, Lucy! You have accomplished much of what you set out to do, but you haven't learned the most important lesson. You are fine just the way you are. Humans aren't meant to fly. Just be your precious You."

"I didn't know," said Lucy blushing. "I guess I was stupid to think I could let go of my feet to fly."

Praying Mantis continued, "It's OK to make mistakes or not know things—you are not stupid. You are still learning. I know you did your best. It was resourceful and creative of you to stuff all your feelings into your backpack until you were ready to deal with them. It was clever to write out things in your journal that you discovered so that you don't forget. You have been working hard to practice these things. It's the only way to grow and learn. All of these gifts have been inside you

the whole time, Lucy. Your friends in the forest have shared how *they* use these skills, but you have to figure out how *you* will use them."

18

Trust That The Universe Cares About You

Lucy thought about all the gifts she had inside of her and smiled. She remembered the Snake and how the process of shedding his skin was itchy and uncomfortable. He also trusted that there would be a new skin waiting for him when he got out. He was very confident.

Lucy stated confidently, "I can use my confidence to trust in my Self. No matter what I am feeling, it will gradually move through to a new understanding that will help guide my way."

She looked at Bird, who could soar high to see the entire forest when sometimes we get too focused on just one tree. She lived in the moment and had an intuition about where to push because she was more of a doer than a thinker.

Lucy said, "I can use what I have learned and experienced to see more clearly. I have choices about how to get my needs met, and it's important to take risks to try."

Lucy took a moment to admire her friend, the Butterfly, who was securely perched on her finger. She was once a beautiful striped Caterpillar and hid away to keep herself safe. Even though she was scared of what was happening and in terrible pain, she stayed curious about what remarkable changes were taking place. She didn't give up, and she wasn't afraid to tell others what she needed. Lucy decided that she could do those things, too. Lucy stated firmly, "I will tell people how I feel and ask for what I need. I can trust that I will figure a way to get through anything that comes my way!"

She remembered her friend, the easy-going Worm. He was so sure of his worth and voice and did not feel the weight of the soil on top of him. He gave what he could to the soil to provide nutrients. She rested her head on the soft earth and listened intently. She was sure she could hear him gently encouraging the seeds to spring forth and follow the warmth and affection of the sun.

Lucy was determined and said, "I can use my sense of calm and caring to reassure myself. I can make sure to give my Self things that are nourishing. I can also encourage others to learn from Terrible Things and spring forth in their own way. I will honor my friend the Worm by sharing what I know."

She took a big s-n-i-f-f of her pansy. She recalled her friend, the Snapdragon, who took a great risk. She cherished all the flowers who took risks to bloom, show their true colors, and share their scent with her.

Lucy declared, "I will use my courage to show my true Self, even if I don't know what will happen. I will risk sharing my Self with others, even if I make them sneeze and wheeze!"

She looked most thankfully at Ladybug. He had been so patient to stick by her through this whole journey, even when she was having a hard time and feeling unpleasant. He had been so in tune with her feelings and taught her to trust what she was feeling and to listen with no judgment.

Lucy promised, "I will be loyal to my Self and listen to the wisdom of what my body and feelings are telling me. Instead of judging my feelings as being right or wrong, I can be curious about what they might be trying to tell me. I will also be compassionate and patient with my Self when venturing out into the unknown…and be open to changing and growing.

19

A Magical Transformation

Just then, a flittering sound arose in the distance. It grew louder and louder. Humming and flittering. "What is it?" Lucy asked.

"Shhh," hushed Praying Mantis. "The Butterflies are coming!"

They all watched in amazement as the sky was suddenly filled with moving colors fluttering about. Fantastic radiant blacks and orange and whites and wines—reds and orange and yellow and indigo. It was exhilarating watching thousands of Butterflies dancing in the sky. Lucy fell into an amazing spell, gently swaying back and forth. Although her feet were firmly weighted to the ground, she too was dancing with the Butterflies. She was not connecting the dance with the Terrible Thing that had happened. Her mind was filled with thousands of Butterflies. Her backpack flew open and released all the contents into the sky. Tears of liberation streamed down her face. She looked at her Self in the reflection of her tears and saw she had changed, too. She liked what she saw in her reflection. Even though the Terrible Thing would always be a part of her, she no longer felt so weighed down by it. She no longer had to carry the heavy burden.

"You forgot something important about Ladybugs, Lucy," said Praying Mantis.

"What's that?" asked Lucy.

"Well," replied Praying Mantis, "Ladybugs taste awful, but they are also very lucky to have around. They love unconditionally. When you see one, it means someone who loves you is thinking of you."

Lucy began to remember all the important people who might be thinking about her back home and she understood what she needed to do. "I will remember all of you," said Lucy. "Thank you for teaching me what was in my heart from the very beginning. I will miss you all terribly."

They assured Lucy that anytime she wanted to visit, they could be found anywhere that nature lives.

20

*Lucy Finds Her *Self**

Lucy paused for a second and looked at her journal. Caressing its worn edges, she felt more free and lighter than she ever had before. Yes, she could fly, but not like a Bird, Butterfly, or Ladybug. She could fly like no other creature could. She could fly freely into her experiences. She could take risks and was not afraid to go into the unknown. Her soul was flying to her inner sky.

She felt like the Snake peeling off his skin. She could let go of her journal now. She remembered the Worm who lost half of his body and could regenerate. It was time to depart from her journal friend that she carried during this time. She took her journal back to the safe protective cover of the furry tree. Now, it was time to bury it under the tree, which could protect and guard it for her. She could bury it, creating a sacred place. She knew that when the spring would come, many sprouts would grow from her sacred place and show off their beautiful colors and wisdom from her diary.

She ran down the hill, screaming from within, "I am free! I am free! Now, I trust myself! I trust my existence! I trust my wisdom! I trust my being! I trust my body! Now, I do not need my journal to remind me anymore. I trust my Self! My whole being is a reminder. My body is my journal. My life is my journal. Yes, I am free. Now, I can fly like a Butterfly. My feet are not stuck anymore. I feel light. I let go. I let go of my cocoon!"

Lucy realized that the crack was not in the wall. The crack was in her shell. And, she was curious to pass through it. In the end, curiosity killed the Caterpillar. However, a beautiful and colorful Butterfly was born.

Lucy's story was paradoxical. She had to lose her Self in order to find her true Self.

The End…and a new beginning.

21

Lucy's Journal

- Find a private space to sit quietly
- Feel the good life affirming energy surrounding me
- List out names of important people who love me
- Remind myself that I am loved
- Remember happier times
- Hug my Self
- Smell the fresh air

* Be aware of different sounds around me—listen carefully
* Feel the grass with my hands—feel the temperature and its softness
* Remind myself to breathe and that it's going to be OK
* Beware of Terrible Things (Praying Mantis)
* Keep practicing karate
* Be aware of what I'm feeling in my body
* It's important to notice what feels good

* Do things that feel good to take gentle care of myself
* Remind myself that I am not alone
* Remember to B-R-E-A-T-H-E
* More heads are better than one
* I can yell to someone I trust for help
* Trust what my body is saying
* Be curious about what the feeling is trying to tell me
* Talk about my feelings with someone I can trust
* There are different ways to cope with Terrible Things

* Try not to worry too much
* Listen to what my body signals are saying and trust I'll know what I need
* When I feel uncomfortable in my skin, I can use moisturizer with Aloe
* Have a nice bath in cool water
* Move my body
* Make a sound out loud (like hissing or saying Eww or Yucky Blech!
* When the unpleasant feelings come, trust they will pass
* It's OK to ask for help

* Be strong and ask questions, even if feeling intimidated
* It's good to help others
* Share what you know
* Let others share what they know
* Find balance and stability
* Remember to say thank you
* Don't give up
* Concentrate and focus on what I want to happen
* Show off a little
* Sing loudly
* If I am angry I can stomp my feet and yell

- I can ask the one I am angry with to back off
- Vent to somebody about why I am angry
- I cannot hurt myself or someone else
- I can hit, kick, or throw my backpack (as long as there's nothing breakable)
- I can make angry sounds and angry faces
- Find compassion for others
- Be willing to consider forgiveness

* If I have a problem with someone, I should try to work it out with them directly
* Remember to eat healthy and tasty things
* Recognize my beauty
* Try to stay curious about what is happening
* Be compassionate and kind
* It's OK to tell others I can't talk right now
* Respect the need for privacy for both your Self and others
* Be patient

* Remember to laugh loud and play
* Try to be spontaneous
* Learn new words
* Be creative like nature
* Stop to smell the flowers and other things around me
* Name all the different things I notice and see
* Use my energy to keep pushing forward even when it's dark
* Feel the warmth of the sun on my face
* Be brave and courageous

* Risk showing my true self, even if it's different from others
* Trust that I am important in my own special ways
* Imagine breathing all the negative energy out of the part of my body that hurts
* It's important to be able to laugh at my Self
* It can be good to let others learn how to do things on their own
* Remember to take rests
* S-T-R-E-T-C-H my body

What other things would you like to add?

Tamara Steinhubl

Curiosity Killed the Caterpillar

Tamara Steinhubl

Curiosity Killed the Caterpillar

Curiosity Killed the Caterpillar

Tamara Steinhubl

Curiosity Killed the Caterpillar

Tamara Steinhubl

Curiosity Killed the Caterpillar

Tamara Steinhubl

Curiosity Killed the Caterpillar

Curiosity Killed the Caterpillar

Tamara Steinhubl

Curiosity Killed the Caterpillar

Tamara Steinhubl

Curiosity Killed the Caterpillar

Made in the USA
Charleston, SC
21 May 2011